The Booger Book

The Adventures of Milo Snotrocket

J.B. O'Neil

Published by J.J. Fast Publishing LLC

The Booger Book

Table of Contents

For my son Joe, who loves to laugh about completely disgusting stuff like boogers, farts, barf, poop, snot, and pee...Enjoy!

FREE BONUS – Ninja Farts Audiobook

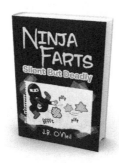

Hey gang...If you'd like to listen to the hilarious audiobook version of my fart-tastic new book "Ninja Farts – Silent But Deadly," you can download it for free for a limited time by going online and copying this link: http://funnyfarts.net/

Enjoy!

Don't ever flick your boogers randomly off into space...

Ever seen a shooting star? Well I saw one in the back yard with my Dad the other night, and he told me that if I made a wish right then it would come true (ha...like that really works). I wonder if my Dad would still want me to make a wish if he knew what these shooting stars REALLY were though. I know this is totally true because I read it in my science book...did you know that those crazy stars are actually huge flaming balls of boogers flicked into outer space at the speed of light?

I mean think about it...have you ever SEEN your boogers ever again after you send them shooting off your middle finger? Not me. I think that is seriously cool, but I have just one question: what do the astronauts do with all of those flaming snot-balls up in space? Windshield wipers don't work very well a zillion miles up in the air, and I bet even creepy alien spacecraft are afraid of these extra-terrestrial Booger Storms.

NEVER wipe your boogers under your desk at school...

If your school janitor is anything like ours, you should never ever wipe your warm, fresh boogers on the underside of your desk. "Rrrrrrrrrevolting little booger boy" is what Mr. Fizzlewizzle called me when he came in to complain to my teacher about the amazing stash of boogers I had been storing under my desk. He said it really loudly too, so loud that everyone in the class heard. Now those two meanest girls in the whole school (Stacey and Lacey Splatterpop) chase me around at recess calling me "Boogerboy...boogerboy...boogerboy!" It's just so embarrassing.

The worst part of it all though is that Mr. Fizzlewizzle scraped away every last one of my precious boogers, and actually scrubbed the underside of my desk smooth and clean. Dang!..that took me 3 months of digging and wiping, and now my entire booger collection is GONE!

Avoid adding them to your bowl of corn flakes at breakfast...

Have you ever been late for school? Well I have, and I blame boogers-coated cornflakes. Here's what happened...I was really tired of the way my stupid old cornflakes tasted, so I decided to add something extra special to my bowl of boring cereal. I picked a couple delicious nuggets out of my shnozzeroo, rolled 'em up good and tight, and then dropped them in one by one into my bowl of crispy yellow flakes. I added some milk, stuffed a couple spoonfuls into my pie-hole and began to chew. And chew. And chew. Yeah, who knew? Mixing 128 corn flakes, 7 green boogers and a little milk makes a chewtastic goop that can make you late for school.

"Hurry up you're going to miss the bus!" my Mom yelled from upstairs. And sure enough...I watched the school bus roll right up to the end of our driveway, open and close that dumb folding door, and then pulled away while I was still chewing my new favorite breakfast. I chewed until I thought my teeth were actually going to pull right out of my head. Maybe I won't roll those boogers so tight next time, or else let them soak a little longer in the milk before I scarf them down for breakfast.

Collecting them in a jar to give to your Grandma is a big mistake...

Have you ever seen your Grandma without her teeth? I have, and believe me...it's not a pretty sight. It's terrible in fact. You see, last summer my Grandma gave me a big jar of pickled cucumbers from her garden to take home to my Mom (yuck!). Then my mom sent me back over to grandma's house with a big jar of brussel sprouts from *her* garden (double yuck!). I figured that as long as she likes to eat green stuff, I might as well fill the jar with some home-grown produce that she'll really never forget. So I emptied out the icky sprouts and stuffed the jar with a couple handfuls of boogers that I harvested from the top-secret stash in my closet.

19

Anyway, she took one look at these all-natural treats that I brought her, opened the jar, grabbed a whole handful of boogers and stuffed them into her mouth. She chewed once...chewed twice...and then stopped chewing completely. Nothing happened then for like 10 seconds, and then she spit out that big half-chewed booger-wad so hard that her false teeth flew out of her mouth, sailed across the room and bit her parrot in the butt! Needless to say, Polly the Parrot was pretty surprised!

Decorating cupcakes with beautiful booger decorations is not advisable ...

Okay I was feeling pretty inspired after watching "Master Cupcake Champions" on cable TV the other night, and then I had a brilliant idea. I dug around in my nose and pulled out a couple dozen winners, and used food coloring to turn them into a beautiful and crunchy topping for cupcakes. Obviously these were the most awesome cupcake decorations I had ever seen, and so I sprinkled them on a plate of fresh cupcakes that my Mom had made for my school bake sale.

When my Mom took them to school the next day, they looked so tasty and delicious that she sold all of those amazing booger treats in 15 minutes flat! Unfortunately almost everybody returned these amazing cupcakes wondering why they tasted so salty...or at least that's what witchy Mrs. Wartface said when she demanded all her money back (plus extra money for "damages"). My Mom was pretty sad and had absolutely no idea what happened, but not me though. I ate all of those delicious little booger-cakes in the car ride home.
Mmmmmmm...I guess boogers are an acquired taste.

Smearing them on your Dad's reading glasses is a serious disaster...

Okay, not only do I think camping is a total waste of time, but it's also completely boring! I hate stupid camping! So last Saturday I smeared a particularly dark and hairy boogie on my Dad's sunglasses when we were driving out to Moose Tongue State Park to go ice fishing out in the freezing cold. I'll admit it...that was a big mistake. Because when we got out of the car he put on his sunglasses and started SCREAMING at the top of his lungs, "Bigfoot! Bigfoot! Run son it's a big hairy Bigfoot monster!" And then he took off at top speed into the woods.

Of course, he couldn't outrun that big hairy booger that I had smeared on his shades...which I guess must have looked a little bit like a giant snotty monster to my Dad so close up like that. Well at least we didn't have to spend the rest of the weekend in a dumb tent, but the Park Rangers weren't too happy trying to talk my Dad out of a tree.

Sticky ones are surprisingly useless for hanging art projects on the fridge...

I like to think of myself as the little problem solver around my house, so when we ran out of scotch tape to hang my awesome zombie alien drawings on the refrigerator door, I had to think fast. Hmmm....What else is really good at sticking stuff together? Slimy snotballs of course! So I gave it a try the other day. I pulled only the biggest, juiciest boogers out of my nose, placed them carefully onto the back of each drawing, and stuck them onto the shiny stainless steel door of the refrigerator.

My plan was working great for about 24 minutes, but then I made an important scientific discovery: cold temperatures dry boogers out! So all my amazing works of art just pulled right off the refrigerator door and ended up all over the kitchen floor.   Oh well...all in the name of science. I bet even Albert Einstein had some days when his booger experiments didn't work out like he had planned.

Why my Mom's new tablet is off limits to booger boy...

Boy I love my Mom's cool new tablet gizmo, and believe it or not this slick little screen makes an awesome home for boogers! Here's the amazing thing: unlike the refrigerator door, your boogers don't freeze up and fall off. No way...in fact, I'm really surprised at how well they always stick to this cool tablet thingee. They stick and stick and then stick some more. In fact, from my testing they may actually be best place ever to leave them, right there on that shiny little screen.

But my Mom doesn't agree. She went red and blew steam out of her ears the day I did that to her new tablet. I even tried to tell her that I didn't do it on purpose. I didn't know that I had a sticky snotglob on my pointy finger when I played a game on it...until it was too late and the screen was covered with nosegunk after the bonus round. In fact, I think a sticky booger-finger may actually give you an unfair advantage playing video games, because I beat my high score by 17,648 points!

Wiping nose-candy on the principal's doorknob is usually frowned upon...

I call my principal "Mr. Wobblegobble" because he has like twenty-two chins which jiggle around like jello pudding whenever he gets mad. I know this because I end up in his office a LOT, and it's never because I've won a fantastic price for the best handwriting in class. This week I got sent there at the end of the day to discuss the "Booger-Desk Incident", and as usual I had to sit in this dumb chair outside his office for like 47 minutes.

I was actually starting to feel a little nervous sitting there for such an extra-long time...And when I get nervous, I start digging in my nose. EUREKA! In no time I pulled out a booger about as big as my nose itself, and then I heard the last bell of the day...and I knew I was SAFE! Whoo-hoo! Time to go home! But before I left Mr. Wobblegobble's smelly little office, I wiped my sticky green prize on the door knob to his office. You gotta love being saved by the bell.

Dad won't like it if you push boogers into his computer keyboard...

Would you believe that when you try to type <u>A Serious Report about Bio-Tech Stock Evaluations</u> on a booger-filled keyboard, it turns out completely different from what you expected? It's completely true. "Rising stock shares" (blahblahblah) comes out as "Purple monkey bottoms..." Can you believe that my Dad tried to blame ME for this technical malfunction because I happened to push some boogers in between the letters on his computer keyboard?

It's true...he sent me to my room. Bet my Mom said it was HIS fault for not reading through his Very Important

Report properly before he sent it to the Big Boss that he works for. And I tried to tell him the main reason the letters f, l n, t and p were sticky is because of the glass of orange juice that I spilled on his laptop, NOT the boogers stuck between the keys. At last, a disaster that couldn't be blamed on boogers! My Dad still isn't convinced though...

Totally do not use boogers as freckles on your sister's Secret Princess Dolls...

Okay, I admit it. Sometimes I end up in my little sister's bedroom and I pick up some of her Secret Princess Dolls. Not to play with them of course, but because I think I can make them even more beautiful than they already are. For instance, there are no freckles on them. Who ever heard of a doll without some cute little freckles? It just doesn't make sense.

So one day I decided to help my sister out with her homely little dolls, and I gave them all some new beauty marks: tiny little green and brown freckles that I dug out of my nose. I thought they all looked like Miss America, but for some reason my sister didn't agree and she started screaming at the top of her lungs. I mean, she totally loooost it. Her sobs became screams, and then the screams turned into howls. And then all the dogs in the neighborhood started howling too, until there was such a terrible noise that somebody called the cops.

Boy, my Dad's red face when he tried to explain that all the fuss was about boogers. "Only boogers! It was only boogers!" he kept saying to the cops when they showed up at our front door. When I added "Yup, only boogers!" they all stared at me in that really mean way, you know the one that makes you wish you had a fresh supply ready to flick?

My dinner specialty? Spaghetti with booger-balls of course...

I'm a pretty good cook and I like to give my Mom a hand in the kitchen whenever I can. Spaghetti with booger-balls is my specialty, and it's really easy to make! Here's the recipe:

Step 1: Have your Mom cook up a big pot of delicious homemade spaghetti sauce.

Step 2: Wait for her to leave the room or until she starts fussing with your baby brother.

Step 3: Harvest a handful of fresh booger balls from your nose and add them to the boiling pot.

Step 4: Let this special sauce simmer for 2 hours to allow them to completely flavor the sauce.

Step 5: Serve piping hot over a bowl of spaghetti and wait for the compliments to start pouring in from your grateful family. It really doesn't get any better than spaghetti with booger-balls on Sunday night!

You should certainly never, ever stick them on the inside of your car window...

So we were supposed to write an essay about car safety in English class... I got a D+ and my teacher told me "This was not a creative writing assignment young man!" I don't get it...this is all totally true...you be the judge:

"Why is it dangerous to stick fresh boogers on the inside of your parents' car window? Simple...because it'll probably make your Mom's head explode! And do you have any idea what exploded brains DO when they meet the snotty booger slime on your car window? No? Well, let me tell you...they combine to make giant alien slugs...Big as your foot, with booger-loving brains. And the very next time you go on a trip, there they will be: under the car seat waiting for you. You could make friends with them, if you want to, but I have to warn you - they smell bad. Really bad, like that forgotten sweaty sock that's been living under your bed for the last three months. But if you can put up with that awful smell, they will follow you everywhere, just as long as you keep feeding them boogers!"

Health Warning: DO NOT stuff your boogers back into your nose...

Picture this: you have just fished an enormous blue-ribbon booger out of your nose during study hall, and as you sit there admiring its remarkable size and color, the librarian starts walking towards you with that "you're in big trouble mister" look on her face. So what do you do? Well your first thought may be to hide the evidence and stuff that juicy booger right back where it came from.

Okay, this is VERY IMPORTANT: no matter how tempting it is, do not EVER under any circumstance attempt to stick that big boogie back into your nose again. You nose is an exit, not an entrance, and this practice goes against all laws of nature. You see there's only enough room for just the right amount of boogers in there, and the moment that you pull one out, another one quickly grows to take its place. And if you just keep removing them and stuffing them back, extra boogers will start to grow out of your ears like slimy green ferns. And then you'll end up picking your EARS every day as well as your nose just to keep up with the never-ending supply of boogers...But wait a minute...that doesn't sound like such a bad idea now...

Blowing bubbles with a big wad of boogers is a bad idea too...

I go through a lot of bubblegum. I'm a bubble-blowing champion actually because I can blow bubbles bigger than any kid on my block. Everybody tries to beat me but I can always blow a bubble bigger than my head and kick their butt in a contest. One time I was walking down the street and Jimmy Monkey-face's little brother challenged me to a steel-cage death match bubble blowing contest.

Now I was completely out of bubble gum, but I wasn't going to let that stop me! So I tried something new: I dug around in my shnozz and pulled out a huge snotball, popped it in my mouth and started working it into a big wad of booger-gum. Jimmy Monkey-face's little brother looked on helplessly as I started blowing that huge wad of boogers into the biggest bubble I've ever blown...bigger...bigger...bigger...until it was twice as big as my head.

That disgusting bubble was green and brown with big nose-hairs sticking out of it, and as I watched it in amazement with my eyes crossed I knew exactly what was going to happen next. It was going to pop...and then it did. BAM! Filthy nosegunk flew everywhere and splattered Jimmy Monkey-face's little brother right in the face with sloppy snotty booger-gum. Nobody challenges me to a steel-cage death match! I always win these things...

Do not store them on a "Booger Wall" next to your bed...

Who needs wallpaper when you can decorate the walls of your bedroom with boogers? I mean think about it: you're sitting in bed picking your nose, pull out a winner, and then what? Well at that point you've got 3 choices:

1. You can put it in a tissue and throw it the waste basket (yeah RIGHT...)

2. You can flick it away into the darkness of your bedroom (where it will just get be lost in the carpet somewhere or fly off in to space like we talked about), or

3. You can just reach over and wipe it on the wall so you can check it out in the morning.

Of course I prefer a booger-wall. I've been working on mine for 7 months now, and it's totally awesome...it's practical...it's convenient...it's cool-looking...and it'll keep your little sister out of your bedroom forever.

Never put booger in the salt and pepper shakers at a restaurant...

I hate eating out with my family. I get really bored while my sister eats one pea at a time, and we all have to wait for her to finish. What is it with peas anyway? Give me a good old booger any day...they're much tastier than stupid peas and they grow a lot faster too. That's what gave me the idea for making the food taste better at The Gobbler Grill, the restaurant I go to with my family every Friday night.

Well, I should say it's the restaurant that we USED to go to. My Dad says we're never going there again, after they caught me generously sharing my boogers with the other customers by dropping a single boogie into all of the salt and pepper shakers. Honest, I was only trying to be helpful! But the owner of The Gobbler Grill didn't seem to see it that way, and now we'll have to find another favorite restaurant because he told my Dad that he won't let us eat there anymore. That's fine with me...what kind of restaurant doesn't have boogers on the menu anyway?

You can use boogers in art class...nobody will know the difference.

Who need modeling clay when you've got the best building material in the world right in your nose? They could have built the Pyramids out of boogers actually and they would probably last even longer. That's how I see it anyway, and that's exactly what I used for my last art project: a big hunk of sticky nose-gunk. The assignment was to create a beautiful animal sculpture and I decided to do a beautiful booger-giraffe. This project required a bit more boogers than I had up my nose at the time, so I brought some into school the next day in a shoebox from my secret stash at home. I shaped it into the coolest-looking giraffe that I've ever seen.

Other kids painted their animals different colors, but I left mine a natural dark green that dried super-hard in the kiln with the other stupid clay animals. My art teacher asked me how I got that awesome color, and I told him sorry buddy...an artist has some secrets that can never be shared.

Cramming them into the end of your sister's flute can be truly horrible...

Believe me...you never, ever, EVER want to stuff boogers into the end of your sister's flute. Take my word for it on this one. If you cram boogers into the end of this already horrible-sounding thing, the next time she takes a deep breath and tries to play it, all that will come out will be an incredibly horrible screeching sound.

I can't even describe how terrible this noise is. It's worse than the sound of a dozen starving monkeys chewing on your pet guinea pig. It sounds worse than all the hours you've ever heard her practice Jingle Bells on her flute in July, worse than the time she howled when you freckled

49

her dolls with your perfectly placed boogers.   In fact, the horrible sound that comes out of your sister's booger-stuffed flute sound will make you want to hide under your bed for days. So just don't even think about it, okay? Nuff said.

Smearing them on your little brother's glasses results in screaming...

Did you know that glasses make things look bigger? MUCH bigger? Well, I do now, and so does my little brother Stanley. And apparently it's <u>all my fault</u> that after I mushed a big green glob of nose-candy onto his nerdy looking glasses, my little brother ran screaming through the house about the space monster coming after him. And then Stanley the dork stepped on the cat...and things started to go downhill from there.

Because then the cat scratched the dog, who snapped at my sister, who fell backward into my Mom, who slipped and dropped an entire mega-sized bowl of strawberry

Jello into my Dad's lap, who finally turned around and hollered at ME. I mean, I don't think it fair at all. How was I supposed to know he was going to wear a brand new suit to work that day?

Never play Angry Birds on your Dad's cell phone after picking your nose...

Now my Dad's usually pretty cool, even though he goes bonkers every now and then when I ask him a million questions. But the one time I saw him get REALLY angry was when I accidentally left just one or two or three teeny weeny baby boogerettes on the screen of his cell phone. I mean really...how's a kid supposed to know that fancy cell phones with touch screen technology don't work with small deposits of dried snot on the screen?

If they can land a man on the moon and make 92-inch televisions, how come they can't invent a phone that you can play Angry Birds on after picking your nose? Come to think of it, if they can make a game that flings birds at targets, surely a little nose-crud shouldn't cause any problems at all, right?

Feeding booger food to your goldfish makes them freaky...

I used to have goldfish. Four of them actually: Plink, Plonk, Tink and Tonk. Well I actually STILL have four fish called Plink, Plonk, Tink and Tonk, but now they're more like "greenfish". Here's why: one day last week I ran out of fish food. It was Sunday night and the pet store was closed, and my orange little friends looked really hungry. So I came up with what I thought was an awesome idea: I picked a couple green prizes out of my nose and dropped them into the bowl. They swam up to the top of the bowl as soon as these tasty treats hit the water and gobbled them all up in no time.

I was really proud of my awesome plan until I came back an hour later and saw that my goldfish were swimming all wobbly and sideways and they had changed to a cool booger-green color. "Mom's right...you are what you eat" I muttered as I walked by my cool new pets, on my way to feed the dog.

Don't smash boogers into the back of your brother's Legos...

One day my little brother and I decided to build an awesome Space City with his Lego blocks. It was going to be REALLY cool, with towers and landing docks and teleportation devices and all that awesome space-station stuff. We spent an hour building the most important piece of all...a flaming red anti-gravity battle ship that we were going to mount at the top of the good guys' landing pod. But when I tried to click it into place, it wouldn't stick at all.

I got really mad, because these blocks are supposed to stick together...and this was the most important piece! I

57

pushed and pulled and stomped on it, but that flaming red battle ship just wouldn't stick on that darn landing pod. But then I remembered: that the last time that my little brother made me mad, I spent an afternoon pushing hard little boogers into the backs of all his red Legos. And as I slowly turned over the red space ship, I saw a solid block of petrified boogers staring back at me. I looked at my brother and he looked at me, and then I said: "I'm tired of this stupid game...let's go watch some TV Stanley!"

Booger candies for Valentine's Day doesn't seem to work...

Okay, I'll admit it...I had a big crush Francine Bricklebacher. She's the freckle-faced girl who sat 4 seats away from me in English class. I had been staring at every little freckle on her cute button nose for ages, and I just couldn't wait to give her a super-special gift on Valentine's Day. Now I know that most kids usually bring stupid little cards to class with candies glued to the back on Valentine's Day.

But that's dumb.

Anybody can do that. I wanted to give Francine a REALLY special present that she'd always remember. So on Valentine's Day I left a big box of homemade heart-shaped booger candies on her desk along with a mysterious note saying "From your secret admirer". Well you won't believe what happened next...she stomped right on over to me and slammed down all those beautiful booger hearts on my desk and told me that she's never, ever going to speak to me again. I don't think I'll ever understand girls!

Detention forever if you stir them into your teacher's salad at lunchtime...

My teacher Mrs. Wigglebottom sits at her desk every day at lunchtime and eats a big green salad with lots of gross-looking vegetables in it. Yuck! How can she eat that every day for lunch? So I decided to add a special secret ingredient to her rabbit food, and I sprinkled a dozen crispy little boogers on top of her salad before I left for the cafeteria. They looked just like bacon bits actually, but were probably even tastier. When I got back from lunch I asked her in my most helpful voice, "So how was your delicious salad today Mrs. Wigglebottom?"

Well her face turned as red as a rotten tomato and she told me that I'm going to be staying after school for detention today, tomorrow, and the next day...in fact, I think I'll be in detention EVERY day for the rest of my life. I think that's not fair at all. I mean when I'm a giant like my Dad, how are my knees going to fit under my school desk? And besides, I was only trying to help -- salad is really just so disgusting!

Sticking one on your pencil when your eraser wears out just doesn't work...

"What have you done to your homework?!" my Mom screamed. "Nothing Mom..." I told her, but that wasn't exactly the truth. You see the eraser on the end of my pencil wore out, so I stuck a booger on there instead. It seemed like a really good idea at the time, but when I wrote "23-9 = flesh-eating space monster" and tried to erase it before I got caught, the booger made this really gross-looking green mark all over my homework. And when I tried to rub it out with my dirty fingers, it just made even more of a mess. So finally I stuck out my tongue and tried to lick it all off the page to get rid of the evidence, but this just smeared the boogery slobber all over and made it look even worse. Hmmm...I wonder if I can say the dog ate my homework now...that might work!

Shaking somebody's hand after picking your nose does not win friends...

After freckly Francine stopped talking to me, she made friends with popular Peter. I thought I better make friends with him too if I ever stood a chance with Francine again, so I walked over to him at recess to say howdy.

"Howdy Peter...I'm Milo Snotrocket. Great to meet you."

"Uh...hi Milo. That's a funny name. Why do they call you Snotrocket?"

I raised my right hand to my nose, closed my left nostril, and shot a screaming booger 27 feet into the air. Peter was obviously impressed, so I grabbed his hand and shook it hard. And shook. And shook. "Uh Milo...you can let go of my hand now." Peter said.

But the problem was that I COULDN'T let go, because our hands were actually glued together with the stickiest booger I've ever seen. The other kids came over and tried to help us out, pulling our arms so hard that I thought they might fly off of our bodies with our hands still stuck together with this industrial-strength booger glue. Francine called the teacher on recess duty, who called stupid Mr. Fizzlewizzle.

"Dirrrrrty little booger boy" he snarled as he dripped some slippery gunk on our hands to release them. Now Peter isn't talking to me either. So it just goes to show you: always wipe your hand on your pants before after you blow a 27-foot screaming snot-rocket and shake the hand of a boy that you've never met before so you can get a girl you have a crush on to like you again...

MORE FUNNY FARTS...

If you laughed really hard at The Booger Book, I know you'll love these other stinky bestselling books by J.B. O'Neil (for kids of *all* ages!)

http://jjsnip.com/fart-book

http://jjsnip.com/ninja-farts-book

Did you know cavemen farted?

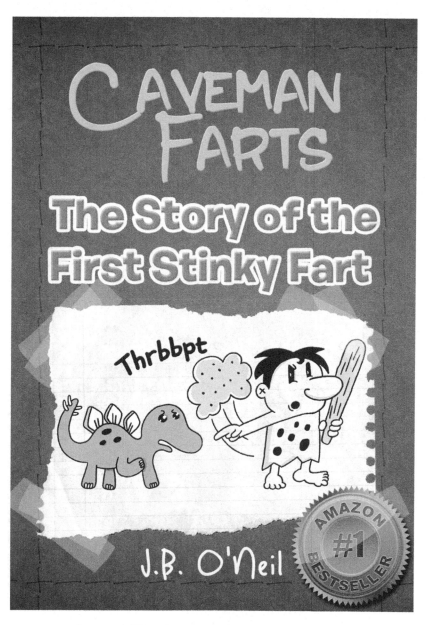

http://jjsnip.com/caveman-farts

A long time ago, in a galaxy fart, fart away...

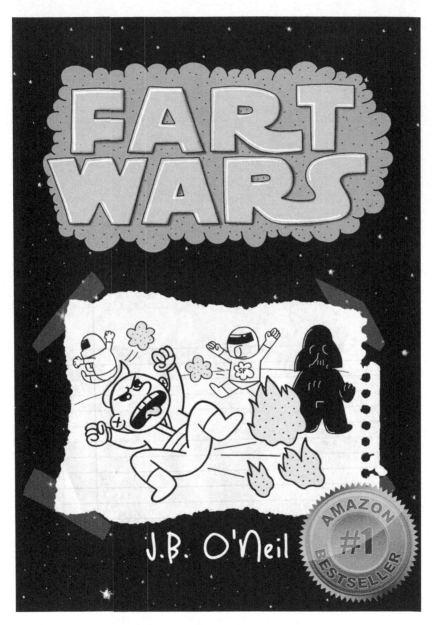

http://jjsnip.com/fart-wars

Think twice before you blame the dog!

http://jjsnip.com/dog-farts

And check out my new series, the
Family Avengers!

http://jjsnip.com/gvz

Made in the USA
Monee, IL
28 April 2021